Andy Shane

and

the Very Bossy

Dolores
Starbuckle

Andy Shane

and

the Very Bossy
Dolores
Starbuckle

Jennifer Richard Jacobson

illustrated by Abby Carter

CANDLEWICK PRESS
CAMBRIDGE, MASSACHUSETTS

For Kent and Tad —for putting up with one bossy sister
J. R. J.

To Carter, Samantha, and Doug
A. C.

First edition 2005

Library of Congress Cataloging-in-Publication Data

Jacobson, Jennifer, date.
Andy Shane and the very bossy Dolores Starbuckle / Jennifer Richard Jacobson ;
illustrated by Abby Carter. —1st ed.
p.   cm.
Summary: Andy Shane hates school, mainly because of a tattletale know-it-all
named Dolores Starbuckle, but Granny Webb, who has taken care of him all his life,
joins him in class one day and helps him solve the problem.
ISBN 0-7636-1940-X
[1. Schools — Fiction. 2. Bossiness—Fiction. 3. Behavior— Fiction.]
I. Carter, Abby, ill. II. Title.
PZ7.J1529An 2005
[E]—dc22   2004057040

2 4 6 8 10 9 7 5 3 1

Printed in the United States of America

This book was typeset in Vendome.
The illustrations were done in black pencil and black watercolor wash.

Candlewick Press
2067 Massachusetts Avenue
Cambridge, Massachusetts 02140

visit us at www.candlewick.com

CONTENTS

1

I Hate School

Andy Shane did not want to be in
school. He did not want to be at
morning meeting. He did not want
to sit up straight on the rug.

He flopped down on his belly
and watched an ant carry a cracker
crumb across the floor. The ant
reminded Andy of his Granny Webb.

Granny Webb loved to catch bugs
and hold them up to the sunlight.
Andy wished that he were at home
catching bugs with her right now.

"Ms. Janice," said a voice like a
squeaky fiddle. "Ms. Janice, someone
is not sitting properly!"

Andy Shane sat up quick. He knew that voice. But Andy's teacher didn't seem to hear it—even though the voice was loud, even though the voice was sitting right in front of her, even though the voice belonged to Dolores Starbuckle.

"This morning," said Ms. Janice, "we're going to find rhyming words. Can anyone tell me two words that rhyme?"

Andy Shane thought of two words: *bug* and *rug*. He looked up. Should he raise his hand?

Other kids were raising their hands. Dolores Starbuckle jumped up and down on her knees and waved her arms like a willow tree in a windstorm. Ms. Janice motioned for Dolores to sit back down.

"Andy," said Ms. Janice. She looked right at him. "Do you know two words that rhyme?"

Andy Shane opened his mouth to tell Ms. Janice the words, but they were stuck in his throat like fruit flies caught in maple syrup.

Ms. Janice waited. The other children waited, too.

"I know two words," called out Dolores Starbuckle. Andy looked at Dolores. "I know two words!" she

yelled. And before Ms. Janice could

call on her, Dolores shouted,

"*Hullabaloo* and *Kalamazoo!*"

Ms. Janice looked surprised.

She smiled. "Yes, Dolores," said

Ms. Janice. "Those words *do* rhyme."

I hate school, thought Andy Shane.

After morning meeting, Andy Shane

looked at a chart on the wall. It was

his turn to go to the math center.

Andy liked the math center. He liked

playing with the fraction puzzles and

the pattern blocks. He liked solving

the tough problems that Ms. Janice

placed there each day. But this morning, Andy wished that he could go to any other center. Yumi was in the math center. Peter was in the math center. And so was Dolores Starbuckle.

Andy Shane decided to work by
himself. He would solve a problem
with pattern blocks. He tried to pull

out the block bin, but it was stuck

on the math shelf. Andy Shane

pulled harder and then harder still.

The container sprang free, but all

the blocks went flying into the air.

"MS. JANICE," yelled Dolores Starbuckle. "SOMEONE IS MISUSING THE MATH MATERIALS!"

2
Being Stubborn

"I don't want to go to school," said
Andy Shane.

"Why not?" asked Granny Webb,
catching a dragonfly on her finger
and holding it close to her nose.

"The *Anax junius*," she said, calling

the dragonfly by its fancy name.

Andy Shane ignored the dragonfly, even though he knew that the *Anax junius* had a bright blue tail, his favorite color. He crossed his arms and said, "I hate school."

"That can't be," said Granny Webb. "Why, Andy Shane, I loved school."

"Well, you didn't have morning meeting when you were in school," said Andy. "And you didn't have math center."

"That's true," said Granny Webb.

"*And* you didn't have Dolores Starbuckle," Andy added.

Granny Webb smiled. "No, Andy Shane, I can't say I did."

So there, thought Andy.

Andy Shane had lived with Granny Webb all his life. When he came into the world, he needed someone who could take good care of him. Granny Webb needed someone to share the fun of hilly woods, salamanders, and stories. So the two of them became a family. Just like that. Andy Shane never longed for more.

"I hear the bus down the road, Andy Shane. Go get your lunch box," said Granny Webb.

Andy Shane didn't move.

"Don't be stubborn, Andy. You have to go to school. You know that."

There was only one person in the world more stubborn than Andy Shane, and that was Granny Webb.

Granny stood up straight.

She put her shoulders back.

She stared at Andy Shane.

She didn't move a muscle.

She didn't blink an eyelash.

She just waited.

"Oh, fine. I'm going," said Andy Shane.

That Granny Webb Stare worked every time.

The bus pulled up, and Andy Shane stepped on. He chose an empty seat and looked out the window at Granny Webb. She looked like she had just stepped on a pricker. Andy thought he must look the same way, too.

3
Granny's Surprise

Andy had no sooner hung up
his sweatshirt in his cubby when
he heard a familiar voice. It was
a voice that Andy Shane would
know anywhere.

It was the voice of his Granny Webb.

"It's a monarch caterpillar," said Granny to the kids who had gathered around her.

Andy came closer.

"Hi, Andy Shane," said Granny. "As I was walking back to the house, I found this caterpillar here. I thought you and Ms. Janice might like to keep it in the science center."

Andy knew that their field was
full of caterpillars, but he was truly
happy that Granny Webb had found
this one.

All the kids wanted to talk to
Granny at once.

"When will the caterpillar turn
into a butterfly?" asked Marcus.

"How long do monarch butterflies
live?" asked Jordan.

"Monarchs migrate all the way to Mexico," said Samantha.

"I like your pockets, Granny Webb," said Polly.

"Ms. Janice, *my* mother told me that visitors can't come to school until October," said Dolores Starbuckle.

"Why don't you join us anyway, Granny Webb," said Ms. Janice. "We're about to have morning meeting."

Morning meeting? Already?
Andy Shane felt like he'd *swallowed*
a caterpillar.

Ms. Janice asked the class to think
of action words—words that told
about *doing* something.

Dolores Starbuckle raised her
hand.

"Yes, Dolores," said Ms. Janice.
"Do you know an action word?"

Dolores stood up and took the
pointer from the board.

"Class, today I will teach you about *verbs*. Verbs are action words," said Dolores. "*Write* is a verb; *read* is a verb, and so is *learn*. Do any of you know an action word?"

No one raised a hand.

Dolores looked at Andy Shane.

"Andy Shane, do you know an action word?"

Andy Shane slunk down on the rug.

"Thank you, Dolores," said Ms. Janice, but Dolores didn't sit down.

"Dolores!" said Ms. Janice. But Dolores had forgotten all about Ms. Janice. She tapped her foot, waiting for Andy to answer.

"I like action words," said Granny Webb. "And I recollect a song with lots of them." Granny stood up and sang, "A mermaid splashed with the fishies in a bay."

Everyone looked at Granny.

"She flipped her tail, and a whale said, 'Hey!'" sang Granny.

"DOES ANYONE KNOW A VERB?" shouted Dolores.

No one was listening. They were all watching Granny Webb dance around the room.

"I SAID—"

Before Dolores could finish her sentence, everyone, even Ms. Janice, began flipping and flopping, twisting and twirling, wiggling and jiggling, and squiggling and giggling.

Everyone, that is, except for Dolores Starbuckle. She was still holding her pointer and gritting her teeth.

1

Beware the Stare

"Come on, Andy," said Granny after morning meeting. "Let's work in the math center."

"It's not our turn," whispered Andy Shane. But before he could

stop her, Granny was in the math

center and she had pulled out all the

pizza puzzle pieces.

"You're not supposed to mix the

pizzas," warned Dolores, coming into

the math center. "You're not supposed

to put the pepperoni with the peppers."

Granny Webb kept making mixed-up pizzas. "I like my pizzas with the works—don't you, Andy Shane?"

Andy Shane stepped back. He knew what was coming.

"MS. JANICE!" yelled Dolores Starbuckle. "SOMEONE IN THE MATH CENTER IS MISUSING THE MATERIALS!"

Andy hoped that Ms. Janice wouldn't hear Dolores, but she heard all right. She came over to the math center to see what was going on.

"Dolores," said Ms. Janice, "Granny Webb isn't misusing the materials; she's using them in a new way."

Dolores Starbuckle's face turned the color of a fire ant. She swept the pizza pieces onto the floor and stomped out of the math center.

Andy and Granny Webb decided to see how the caterpillar liked his new home in the science center. Dolores Starbuckle wandered over, too.

"I'll be the teacher," said Dolores, pointing to a picture on the wall. "What is this, Granny Webb?"

"I believe that that is a *Musca domestica*, Dolores," said Granny.

"Wrong," said Dolores. "This is a picture of a housefly."

"And what is this?" asked Dolores.

"That is a *Photinus pyralis*," said Granny Webb.

"Wrong again!" shouted Dolores. "That is a firefly. Everyone knows that."

"And what is this?" Dolores

pointed to a dragonfly.

Granny Webb didn't say anything.

"What is *this*?" repeated Dolores.

"I'm *waiting!*"

"That is an *Anax junius*," said
Andy Shane. "My Granny Webb
taught me all the fancy names for
bugs, and she knows them better
than anyone."

"OH YEAH?" said Dolores.

"Yeah," he said.

And then Andy Shane did
something he'd never done before.

He gave Dolores Starbuckle the
Granny Webb Stare.

He stood up straight.

He put his shoulders back.

He stared at Dolores Starbuckle.

He didn't move a muscle.

He didn't blink an eyelash.

He just waited.

Finally he asked, "What is this bug, Dolores Starbuckle?"

"Fine," she said. "It's an *Anax junius*."

The Granny Webb Stare worked every time.

"I just remembered that my apples need picking," said Granny Webb. "I'm sorry, Andy Shane. I have to go."

"That's okay," said Andy, smiling.

"Andy Shane, will you teach me the fancy names of these bugs?" Dolores asked.

Andy Shane thought for a
moment.

"*Please?*" asked Dolores.

"All right," said Andy.

Andy told Dolores the fancy name for monarch caterpillar. He told her that soon the caterpillar would build a case called a chrysalis, which was a lot like a cocoon.

"A COCOON?" asked Dolores.

Andy stepped back.

"That rhymes with *cartoon*!" said Dolores with a laugh.

"And *lagoon*!" said Andy Shane. He laughed, too.

"And *baboon*!" said Dolores.

Maybe school isn't so bad, Andy thought. *And maybe, just maybe, Dolores and I can share our rhymes at tomorrow's morning meeting.*